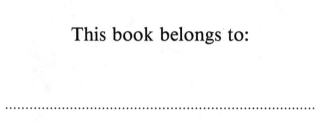

This book belongs to:

....

PUBLISHED BY PETER HADDOCK LIMITED, BRIDLINGTON, ENGLAND.
© FERN HOLLOW PRODUCTIONS LIMITED.

MUDDLES
AT THE MANOR

Written and Illustrated by John Patience

ph

Blodger was the gardener at Trundleberry Manor, and he
was usually very happy in his work, but today he was
feeling sort of restless. The flower beds looked lovely and
the lawns and fountains looked very nice too, but Blodger
felt that he would like to do something really special. The
old rabbit stood thinking for a long time and then suddenly,
as he was looking at the privet hedges, he had a
marvellous idea.

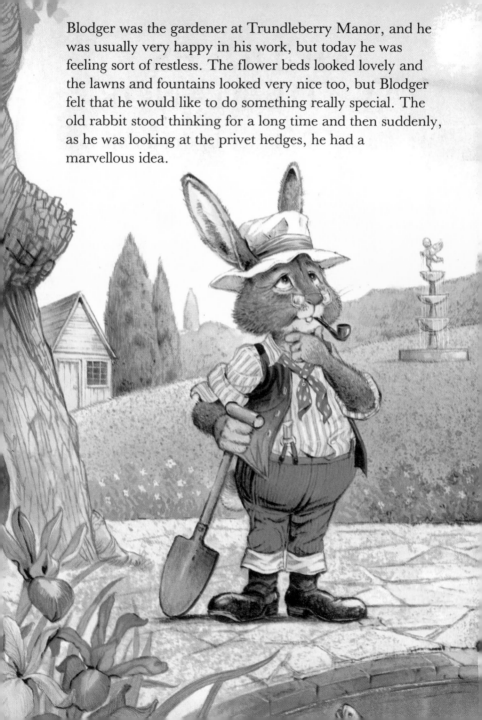

Feeling rather excited, Blodger rushed round to Boris Blinks's bookshop.

"Good morning, Blodger," said Boris. "What can we do for you?"

"I was wondering if you had any books about cutting things out of hedges," replied Blodger.

"Yes of course — you mean 'Topiary'," said the knowledgeable owl.

Boris asked his assistant, Leapy, to bring down a large red book from the top shelf. It was entitled "Teach Yourself Topiary" and was full of beautiful pictures of hedges cut into the shapes of birds and animals. It was exactly what Blodger wanted.

Blodger decided to try something simple first. It was a
rabbit. It looked very nice in the book and in fact it turned
out to be quite easy. Flushed with success, he produced a

row of ducks, a soldier and an elephant! Then he began
working on a giant cockerel. Clip, clip, clip, went Blodger's
shears. Clip, clip, clip. Then suddenly he lost his balance on
the ladder. Clip, went the shears again and down fell the
ladder, Blodger and the giant cockerel. CRASH!

Fortunately for Blodger, Lord Trundle was out in the gardens taking a quiet stroll and heard his cries for help. The poor old rabbit was half buried beneath the giant cockerel, and had broken a leg. Naturally Lord Trundle took Blodger home and quickly telephoned for Doctor Bushy. The doctor put Blodger's leg into plaster, then gave him some very firm instructions. "Well, my dear chap," he said. "There'll be no more topiary for you for a while. You must stay right where you are until your leg gets better."

Because old Blodger was unable to work, Lord Trundle hired Horace Hoppit and Spike Willowbank, who were on holiday from school, as temporary gardeners. The first job Spike and Horace tackled was mowing the lawns. They managed to get the motor mower started quite easily, but steering it was quite another matter.

"Help! Stop it" cried Horace, clinging to the handle of the runaway mower. But it was going far too fast for Spike to catch. It raced crazily around the lawns, ploughed through the flower beds and ended up with a great SPLASH in the middle of a fountain!

Lord Trundle was horrified by the damage which Spike and Horace had done, but he decided to give them a second chance.

"You can make a little fire and burn the garden rubbish," he said.

Now a little fire would have been fine, but Spike and Horace thought it would be much quicker if they made a great big fire and burnt all the rubbish at once, and they built it right next to the potting shed. Well of course, as you might have guessed, the sparks from the fire set the potting shed ablaze.

Lord Trundle lost no time in telephoning the fire brigade,
who quickly arrived on the scene in their big red fire engine
with the bell ringing loudly.

"Stand back!" cried Mr Bouncer, rushing forward with the
fire hose.
A great jet of water shot out of the hose, the fire hissed and
spluttered and sent up great clouds of black smoke. It was a
long battle but at last the two brave firemen put out the
blaze and all that was left was a messy smouldering heap,
which used to be the potting shed.

Spike and Horace got a good telling-off for their silliness, and everyone agreed that it would be a good idea if they didn't make any more bonfires — not even little ones. In fact, Lord Trundle made up his mind to do all the gardening at Trundleberry Manor himself until Blodger's leg was better — and very hard work it turned out to be.

Fern Hollow

MR. CHIPS'S HOUSE

MR. WILLOWBANK'S
COBBLER'S SHOP

MR. CROAKER'S WATERMILL

STRIPEY'S HOUSE

SCHOOL

RIVER FERNY

THE JOLLY VOLE
HOTEL

MR. ACORN'S
BAKERY

MR. RUSTY'S HOUSE

MR. PRICKLE'S HOUSE

POST OFFICE

BORIS BLINK'S
BOOKSHOP

MR. TWINKLE'S
HOUSE

MR. TUTTLEBEE'S
SHOP

MR. THIMBLE'S
TAILOR'S SHOP

WINDYWOOD